GH01018180

Children's Books:
The Witch's Big Night

Sally Huss

Copyright @2014 Sally Huss

All Rights Reserved

ISBN: 0982262590
ISBN 13: 9780982262597

T'was the night of Halloween and all through the house

Every creature was stirring, even the grouse.

The pumpkins were seated on the mantelpiece with care

In hopes that the witch might soon find her way there.

Her presence was all that the evening would need,

As the children would be coming with a great deal of speed.

Knock! Knock came the first little make-believe goblin.

Down the stairs came the witch a-bobblin' and a-hobblin'.

"What do you want?" she yelled, as she opened the door.

"Trick or treat," said the goblin, holding her bag up for more.

"A handful of worms," said the witch with delight.

"Egad!" cried the goblins and ran out of sight.

The next little monster turned out to be

As cute and as funny as a clown could be.

"And, you sir," asked the witch, "what's on your mind?"

"I'd like some candy, if you don't really mind."

"Ha, Ha," laughed the witch, as she stuck her hand in a dish
Then pulled out a handful of smelly dead fish.

"No. No," said the clown as he hurried away.

Said the witch, "I don't understand why these tricksters don't stay."

Next came a lovely crown-covered Cinderella,

Who held the hand of her brother, a prince of a fella.

"What now," sighed the witch? "This is becoming a bore."

"Trick or Treat," yelled the two, when she opened the door.

"Trick or treat, what does that mean if I have nothing for you?

Do you think you can trick me or scare me, you two?"

"We could try," said the prince, trying not to be frightened.

But when the witch offered spiders, his handholding tightened.

Off they ran, leaving the witch to exclaim,

"The world is full of scared-y-cats. It's really quite a shame."

More kids arrived in their Halloween gear

And one after the other ran away in great fear.

Then came a little kid dressed as a skunk.

The witch could hardly open the door; she was in such a funk.

"What's the matter," the little skunk kindly asked?

"No one has tricked me," said the witch.

"Not one has taken on the task."

"I live for Halloween. It's my one night to shine.

All I've been getting are smiley faces at the door all the time."

"I want to see some threats, some meanness, some spunk."

"Perhaps I could help you out," said the kind little skunk.

"What could you do? I'm scary and broody

And as mean as can be.

There's no way someone nice could trick a trickster like me."

"No one can ruffle my feathers.

No one can change me from the way I am.

No one can correct me or upset me.

But still, what's your plan?"

Putting his arm around the witch's shoulder,

The skunk began to speak,

"I'm a little bit hungry. I'm feeling a little bit weak."

"Here, have an apple," said the witch, pointing to

A tub full of apples a-bobbin'.

"Oh, NO!" yelled the witch, as she fell down a-sobbin'.

"You've tricked me. You fooled me into being somewhat nice.

This is the worst kind of worst of all Halloween vice."

"A witch is supposed to be nasty, cruel and unkind."

"Don't worry," said the skunk, "I really don't mind."

With that settled, they both decided to enjoy

The rest of the night,

And by this time they both had an enormous appetite.

Returning to the tub full of apples, they both began to dunk.

And this is how a witch became friends with a skunk.

Yes, Halloween is full of surprises and delights

And happily, every child has a childhood full

Of Halloween nights.

The end,
but not the end
of being kind.

At the end of this book you will find a Certificate of Merit that may be issued to any child who promises to honor the requirements stated in the Certificate. This fine Certificate will easily fit into a 5"x7" frame, and happily suit any child who receives it!

Here is another charming and whimsical book by Sally Huss.

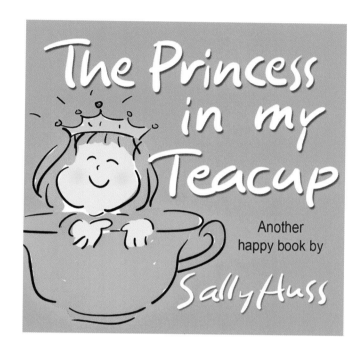

Synopsis: What little girl would not want a princess to visit her? That's what kept happening to the little girl in this story. A princess would show up in a mud puddle, the kitchen sink, a bathtub, and even in a cup of tea. But it is what the princess told her that was most important, and the little girl took it to heart. Who was that princess in her teacup? You'll have to read the book to find out.

All in rhyme and accompanied by over 35 delightfully colorful illustrations that dance along with the story.

THE PRINCESS IN MY TEACUP may be found on Amazon as an e-book or soft-cover book -- http://amzn.com/B00NG4EDH8.

If you liked THE WITCH'S BIG NIGHT, please be kind enough to post a short review on Amazon by using this URL: http://amzn.com/B00O29R3EQ.

You may wish to join our Family of Friends to receive information about upcoming FREE e-book promotions and download a free poster – The Importance Happiness on Sally's website -- http://www.sallyhuss.com. Thank You.

More Sally Huss books may be viewed on the Author's Profile on Amazon. Here is that URL: http://amzn.to/VpR7B8.

About the Author/Illustrator

Sally Huss

"Bright and happy," "light and whimsical" have been the catch phrases attached to the writings and art of Sally Huss for over 30 years. Sweet images dance across all of Sally's creations, whether in the form of children's books, paintings, wallpaper, ceramics, baby bibs, purses, clothing, or her King Features syndicated newspaper panel "Happy Musings."

Sally creates children's books to uplift the lives of children and hopes you will join her in this effort by helping spread her happy messages.

Sally is a graduate of USC with a degree in Fine Art and through the years has had 26 of her own licensed art galleries throughout the world.

This certificate may be cut out, framed, and presented to any child who has demonstrated her or his worthiness to receive it.

Certificate of Merit

(Name)

The child named above is awarded this Certificate of Merit for practicing loving kindness and for being:

*Useful whenever possible

*Grateful at all times

*Friendly to everyone

*Helpful to and Thoughtful of others

Presented by: _____   Date: _____

7989823R00025

Printed in Great Britain
by Amazon.co.uk, Ltd.,
Marston Gate.